# Jamestown Settlement

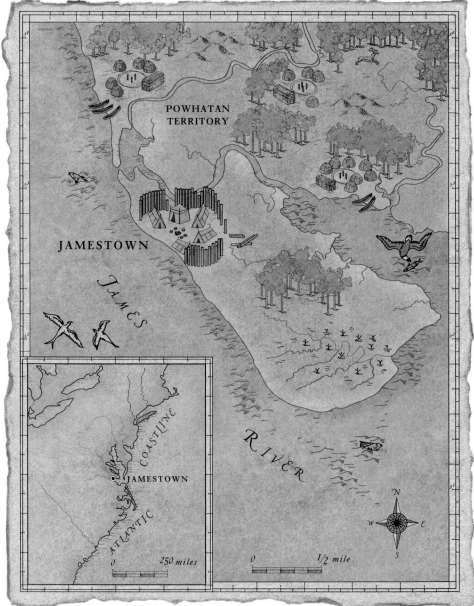

POWHATAN
TERRITORY

JAMESTOWN

JAMES

RIVER

COASTLINE

ATLANTIC

JAMESTOWN

0          250 miles

0          1/2 mile

N
W    E
S

# DISNEY'S POCAHONTAS

## A Boy Across the Sea

by Joanne Barkan

Illustrations by Rachelle and Brooks Campbell,
Lureline Kohler and D. Blakely Fuller

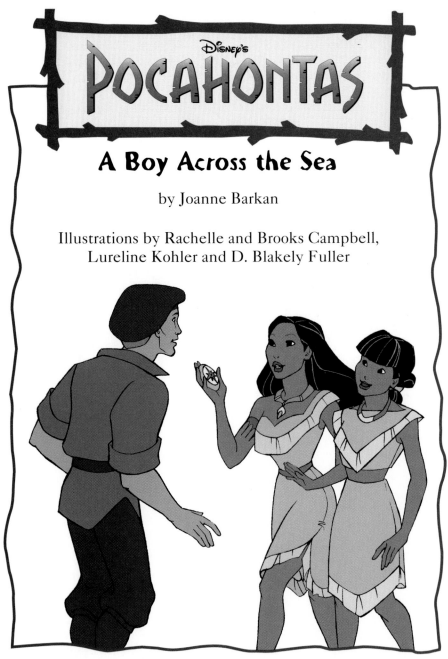

Grolier Books

Published by Grolier Books.
©1995 The Walt Disney Company. No portion of this book may be reproduced without the consent of The Walt Disney Company.
Produced by Mega-Books, Inc.
Design and art direction by Michaelis/Carpelis Design Assoc., Inc.
Printed in the United States of America.

ISBN: 0-7172-8470-0

# CHAPTER 1

Pocahontas, you're not listening!" Nakoma said.

Nakoma and Pocahontas sat side by side on a narrow strip of beach. Water lapped at their feet.

Pocahontas sighed. "I'm sorry. My head is in the clouds today—or across the sea." She looked down at the brass object that lay in her hand. It was a sailor's compass.

"Ah . . . " Nakoma said. "You're thinking about John Smith again."

Pocahontas nodded. "He first showed me this compass exactly a year ago today."

John Smith, an English soldier, had sailed from London with a group of settlers who hoped to find riches across the sea. The settlers landed on the shores where Pocahontas's tribe, the Powhatan, had lived for many hundreds of years.

When fighting between the settlers and the Powhatan broke out, Pocahontas saved John's life and brought peace. John was badly injured in the fighting. He and Pocahontas said farewell, knowing they might never meet again. But they also understood that knowing each other had transformed their lives forever.

Pocahontas put a finger to her lips. "Listen!" she whispered. "Footsteps in the woods. And it's not a Powhatan."

"It's a settler from Jamestown," Nakoma murmured. "No one else would make *that* much noise. Let's hide."

Pocahontas and Nakoma knelt behind

some thick laurel and waited. A few minutes later, a young man stumbled onto the sand. He looked around, bewildered.

Pocahontas laughed and jumped up. "Thomas! Are you lost again?"

Thomas whirled at the sound of her voice. When he saw Pocahontas and Nakoma, he grinned and blushed.

"Yup, did it again," he said. "Thought I was going straight to the settlement. Then I got all topsy-turvy in that forest."

Thomas walked toward Pocahontas and Nakoma. He raised his hand, palm forward, and made a circle in the air. As Pocahontas raised her hand to repeat the Powhatan greeting, Thomas cried out. "That's John Smith's compass! I'd recognize it anywhere." He stared at the instrument and then nodded. "It makes sense that he left it with you."

"What do you mean?" Pocahontas asked.

"You saved his life," replied Thomas.

"Didn't John tell you how he got that compass when he was twelve?"

Pocahontas shook her head.

"It's one of the best stories I've ever heard," Thomas said. "John told it on board the ship from London."

"Will you tell it to us?" Pocahontas asked.

"Sure," Thomas said.

Pocahontas sat down and motioned Thomas and Nakoma to sit beside her.

The three of them faced the water watching the sunlight flicker on the shallow ripples. Thomas cleared his throat and began to speak.

"Well, as I remember the story, it was the month of May in 1592 . . . "

❧

Young John Smith watched the sunlight flicker through the tiny ripples in the glass. He tapped his finger against the pane. *Ra-ta-ta-tat.*

"Glass windows," he whispered. "Real

glass windows in a real inn in the biggest town in England!" He tapped the glass again and said, "John Smith of Willoughby by Alford, county of Lincolnshire, is in *London*!"

John peered into the street. A woman holding two pails stood in front of the inn crying, "Milk-o, cream-o, butter's fine too!" John's stomach grumbled from hunger.

The door to the room swung open. John's father walked in. Behind him was the innkeeper, balancing a pitcher of milk and a plate of bread and cheese on a tray. While the innkeeper placed the food on a long oak table, Mr. Smith hurried to the bed. He gave the lumpy form under the blankets a gentle shake.

"Francis, you should be up and dressed!"

John's younger brother poked his head out of the covers, opened one eye, and mumbled, "Just two more minutes."

John groaned. "That's what he said five minutes ago. And five minutes before that!"

"Come on, Sir Slugabed," Mr. Smith said. "I have business on the docks and then an appointment in the courts at Westminster."

Ten minutes later, Mr. Smith and the two boys were making their way along the crowded street. John's head turned back and forth, and his eyes opened wide. There was so much to see—carts piled high with lumber and bricks, fancy coaches with velvet curtains, basket-men selling root vegetables and herbs, soldiers in uniform, and beggars asking for coins. The iron wheels of the carts clattered against the paving stones.

"Hey," Francis shouted, "can we look at those clocks over there? Can we, Father?"

"Why are you shouting?" John asked.

"Because everyone else is!" Francis

yelled. "It's the best thing about London!"

"I'm not so sure," Mr. Smith said.

"Me either," John muttered. "I didn't know the world could be so noisy. Or so crowded." He ducked between a woman selling flowers and a cart carrying tanned animal hides. "Or so filled with things."

Mr. Smith let Francis stop to look at the watchmaker's gilt clocks and a milliner's embroidered caps and feathered hats. A moment later, Francis pointed to the blue-and-white delftware of a master potter.

"Look at these!" he shouted. "Can we buy something for Mother, Father?"

"We'll shop later on," Mr. Smith said.

"Let's go, Sir Slugabed," John said.

He took Francis's hand and pulled him along. He was impatient to get to the port. He wanted to see the ships—the galleons big enough to sail around the globe, powerful enough to defeat the Spanish Armada, and fast enough to satisfy his idol, the explorer and naval hero, Sir Francis Drake.

In John's imagination, London was not a place to live or even to visit. It was a point of departure. It was the starting place for a life of adventure—*his* life of adventure.

"When do we get to the port?" John asked.

"Around the next corner and straight down the street," Mr. Smith answered.

John dropped Francis's hand and began to run. He weaved between vehicles and passersby.

"John, wait!" his father shouted.

John didn't hear the words. He kept his eyes on the paving stones until he rounded the corner. Then, raising his eyes, he stopped short. "Oh, my!" he whispered. "Look at that!"

# CHAPTER 2

The port of London stretched along the Thames River like a bustling world of its own.

At the center, moored in the middle of the river below London Bridge, were the great sailing ships. Full-rigged galleons with three masts each, they sat tall and motionless in the water. Dozens of small boats ferried cargo, crew, and passengers between the galleons and the quays.

"Look at them!" John said to his father

and brother when they caught up with him. He pointed to the two galleons closest to the bridge. "They're the most beautiful. Where are they from, Father?"

"I'm sure we can find out on the quay," Mr. Smith said. "Let's hurry up, boys."

Mr. Smith found the grain merchants with whom he had business. While he spoke with them, John and Francis studied the ships.

"Was Sir Francis Drake's *Golden Hind* as beautiful?" Francis asked.

"You are curious about the ships?" someone asked in a foreign accent. "*Benissimo.* Perhaps I can help."

John and Francis turned around to face a tall thin man wearing a black velvet hat with a white plume, a black velvet tunic embroidered in silver, and black hose.

"My name is Signor Leonardo Dandolo," he continued. "I believe you were looking at the ship I arrived on." He pointed to one of the galleons. "It is the

*San Marco*. We sailed from Venice."

"Isn't Marco Polo from Venice too?" Francis asked. "Do you know him?"

"*Santo Cielo*, of course not!" Signor Dandolo answered, laughing. "He lived three hundred years ago."

"What cargo does the *San Marco* carry?" John asked.

"Silks, sugar, wines, and spices," Signor Dandolo said.

"And that other ship?"

"The *Bristol*," Signor Dandolo said. "She is English and carries woolen cloth, pewter, tin, and grain."

"Where is she going?" John asked. "And when does she sail? Soon?"

Mr. Smith rejoined his sons. "You're asking too many questions, John," he said softly.

Signor Dandolo smiled. "I must be on my way. But I can tell you that the *Bristol* sails today for Bordeaux, France." He bowed to Mr. Smith. "You have two fine sons, *Signore*. I bid you all *buon giorno*."

Mr. Smith had finished his business. He said to his sons, "Now we'll go to Westminster. We can take a barge up the Thames partway and walk the rest. We should get there in about a half hour."

While they waited for the barge, Mr. Smith and Francis watched a line of swans glide up to the quay. An elderly woman tossed them bits of bread. John watched the *Bristol* for a few minutes. Then he turned to his father.

"I know I'd learn much more at sea than I do in school, Father. On a ship, I—"

Mr. Smith interrupted his son. "John, you're much too young to go to sea. I don't want to have this discussion again until you're at least sixteen and have finished school."

When Mr. Smith saw the disappointment on John's face, his voice softened. "Let's not think about the future right now. I have a surprise for you two."

"What is it?" Francis asked. "Tell us!"

"Well," Mr. Smith said, "tonight we're going to see the best entertainment in London—at the Rose Theater. The company is doing a play called *The Comedy of Errors* by a young actor named Shakespeare. William Shakespeare, I think his name is. I've heard—"

The crowd waiting to board the barge to Westminster surged forward.

"Step lively! Hurry it up, now!" the oarsmen shouted.

Passengers swarmed to the edge of the quay. Sailors, merchants, and tradespeople pushed their way through the crowd.

Mr. Smith took Francis by the hand and warned John, "Stay close to me."

The crowd pressed forward again. John turned to look once more at the *Bristol*. The gilded trim on her stern caught the morning sun.

John stepped back and to the side. He watched the labors of a young sailor hauling bins of grain from the deck down into the hold. Up he climbed and then down he went with another load. Up and down, up and down. . .

Suppose I were that fellow, John thought. I'd sail down the Thames into the English Channel, out to the open sea, and then all the way to the Spanish Indies. Or maybe around the Cape of Good Hope. Or—"

The pushing and jostling had stopped. The crowd on the quay had thinned out. John turned to follow his father. His heart skipped a beat. Francis and his father were gone!

John dashed to the edge of the quay. The place where the barge had been tied was empty. John's gaze swept across and then up the river. He caught sight of the barge. It was passing under London Bridge, heading for Westminster.

# CHAPTER 3

ather!" John screamed. "Francis!"

John put two fingers in his mouth and whistled as loud as he could. At home, the same shrill blast would have echoed around the hills. But in the commotion of London, the sound seemed to melt away.

Father will notice right away that I'm gone, he thought. But the barge won't stop until Westminster. They'll be so worried! Poor Father may think I fell into the river and drowned! They'll take another boat back to look for me. They'll probably look for me at the inn.

John turned and started running toward the stairs that led up to the street.

"I'll go back to the inn," he said. "Sooner or later, they'll be there."

John retraced his steps to the top of the street where he had first seen the port. But beyond that point, he had trouble finding his way. The tall oak-frame houses with sloping tiled roofs all looked the same. So did the crowded streets and twisting alleys. After a while, John admitted to himself that he might be walking in circles without knowing it.

"I can't even ask for help," he murmured. "I was asleep when we arrived, and Father carried me to bed. I don't know the name of the inn."

John asked a shopkeeper for directions back to the quays. He walked to the river thinking about his father and mother, Francis, and his sister, Alice. How long would it be before he was with them again in Lincolnshire?

That's strange, he thought. Until now, I didn't want to go back. I wanted to go to sea. Have I changed my mind? John shook his head. As he approached the river, his thoughts and his steps both quickened.

"Maybe," he said softly, "what happened this morning was meant to happen. Maybe being left behind was a stroke of good luck. Maybe it's a sign I'm supposed to go to sea right away. Today!"

John began to run. When he got to the river, he headed for the quay nearest the *Bristol*. Small boats were still ferrying cargo to the galleon, but now more sailors and officers stood on the quay.

"Excuse me, sir," John said to a seaman. "Where do I apply to join the crew?"

The brawny sailor looked up from the rope he was knotting. "You?" he asked. He threw back his head and laughed.

"Ho, Fletcher!" he called to a bald

sailor. "We have an inquiry."

Fletcher walked over to them.

"Mr. Fletcher here is the *Bristol*'s first mate," the sailor said to John.

John straightened his shoulders, looked Fletcher in the eye, and said, "I'd like to join the crew, sir."

Fletcher glanced at the other sailor and muttered, "How much time do you think I have to waste today?" Then he said to John, "You look like you still belong in school—or maybe in your mum's lap. So get back there."

John didn't budge. "I'm twelve years old. Lots of lads my age go to sea."

"Not on this ship," Fletcher said. "The captain already has a cabin boy, and he's not worth the trouble. Get on home."

John's cheeks flushed. He turned and walked up the quay a few yards. Then he sat down on a trunk. He watched the sailors on the *Bristol* adjust the rigging.

"You want to go to sea, do you?"

The voice startled John. A man with wavy black hair and a purple scar on his cheek sat down next to him.

"How do you know?" John asked.

"Heard you talking to the mate back there," the man said. "Maybe I can help. Jennings is my name."

"Are you on the crew?" John asked.

"Nope," Jennings answered. "I get sick as a dog on the water. But my brother is captain of the *Bristol*. Actually he's my half brother, but we're close as chicks in a nest. If I talk to him for you, he might take you on board."

"Do you really think so?" John asked.

"Look, I can't promise anything. But I can try—if you want."

"Oh, yes!" John said. "Please!"

"I might as well," Jennings said. "But I've got to do this the right way. When my brother gets busy, his temper gets short. And the mate didn't seem to take to you. So it would be better if you stay off the quay for, say, two hours. When you come back, I can have it all set up."

"Thank you!" John said.

"But how do I know you'll come back?" Jennings asked. "Suppose I trouble my brother for you, and then you don't show your face?"

"But I want to go to sea!" John said.

"Well," Jennings said, "have you got anything as security? If I can't get you on board, I'll give it back in two hours. If I make you a sailor, you'll let me keep it."

John stood up. "Yes, of course. That's fair." He took a small leather purse out from under his tunic. Inside was all his spending money—a half crown his father had given him. He dropped the coin into Jennings's hand.

Jennings nodded. "Remember—keep out of sight for two hours. No more, no less."

John hurried to the street. Making sure he would remember the way back, he looked for a watchmaker's shop and checked the time. It was twelve-thirty. The next two hours seemed like the slowest and fastest of his life. John paced the nearby streets, making plans.

I've got to let Father and Mother know I'm fine. I'll be able to borrow paper and pen on the ship. I'll write a letter and post it as soon as I get to Bordeaux.

Thinking of his family made John's eyes smart with tears. But then he pictured a ship on the high seas. *His* ship. The *Bristol*!

At exactly two-fifteen, John started back to the quay. He walked quickly, trying to mark the time. He concentrated on not losing his way. Just as he got to the stairs down to the quay, a church bell chimed the half hour. John raced down the steps two at a time. When he reached the bottom, he looked up.

The *Bristol* was gone.

# CHAPTER 4

John felt the quay sway beneath his feet. The river and the bridge became a blur of color. He took a few deep breaths. His vision cleared. Directly in front of him the water of the Thames was dark, shining, and strangely empty. It was as if the *Bristol* had been only a mirage.

"I've been swindled," John muttered. "Two-timed, hoodwinked, and left without a farthing by that crook Jennings! I can't even buy a crust of bread."

John turned his back to the river and climbed the stairs to the street.

"It's my own fault," he continued. "I was gullible. I know what Father would say. 'You're not ready to go to sea if you get taken like a pigeon by every trickster who comes along.'"

He trudged up the street, still muttering. "I won't be going to sea this year. Maybe I'll never get a chance to go."

John decided he had only one choice—to look for the inn again.

He wandered through the streets, trying not to think about his empty stomach. He was hoping to see something familiar—a shop, a church, anything that would let him know he was near the inn. He tramped up one lane and down another until he entered the square in front of a church.

"Ma'am," he asked a woman passing by, "what church is that?"

The woman turned and stared at John

for a moment as though he had lost his wits. "It's St. Paul's Cathedral, of course. What else would it be?"

John walked around the cathedral, looking at its doors and windows and the central tower, which had no spire. Behind St. Paul's, he found a small courtyard where children were playing a noisy game of tag. He sat down on a stone wall to watch.

"Richard, you're as slow as a fly stuck in molasses!" the biggest boy shouted at the smallest one. "And Anne, you run like a turtle on its back!"

Anne made a dash for the big boy and swiped him on the shoulder. "Caught you, Ben!" she yelled. "Yes, I did, and now you're it!"

Ben scowled and lunged for another boy, who ducked out of the way. He grunted and began chasing the boy around.

"I'm gonna get you, Henry!" Ben shouted. "I'm gonna get you good!"

Henry was fast on his feet. He dodged and changed directions so quickly that Ben couldn't keep up.

"Ben, you can't catch a thing!" Henry cried. "You couldn't even catch that fellow over there. And he's sitting down!" Henry pointed to John.

Ben stared at John. "Who are you anyway? You don't live around here."

John shook his head. "I'm John Smith from Lincolnshire," he said.

Anne started to laugh. "I'm John Smith from Lincolnshire," she repeated. She imitated John's northern accent.

Henry joined in the new game. "Well, I'm Lincoln John from Smithshire. Or maybe I'm Smithy Lincoln from Johnshire. Maybe I don't know who I am, but I'm not from London."

"If you're not from London, you're a country bumpkin," Richard chanted. "That's what my father says."

"Country bumpkin!" Ben yelled. He

skipped a small stone across the pavement. It stopped at John's feet.

"Country bumpkin!" Ben yelled again. He aimed a larger stone at John's feet.

John eyed Ben steadily, but he didn't move. "I am not a country bumpkin."

"Oh, yeah?" Ben answered back. "If you aren't one, then why do you look and sound like one?"

"Aw, leave him alone, Ben," Henry said. "I'd rather play tag."

"Yeah? Well, I'd rather play beat the bumpkin."

The other children looked uneasy, but they didn't speak. John slid off the wall and faced Ben. His arms were at his sides, relaxed but ready.

Ben picked up a heavy stick and waved it over his head.

"Here we go!" he shouted. "Let's have one good game of beat the bumpkin!"

Holding the stick high, Ben took a step toward John.

# CHAPTER 5

John picked up a stone and threw it hard. It slammed into the stick and knocked it out of Ben's hand.

"I challenge any of you to throw like that!" John shouted.

Ben seemed glued to the spot, his arm raised and his mouth open.

"He got you, Ben!" Anne yelled. Then she said to John, "Good throw! Now it's my turn. We'll have a contest."

Henry ran across the courtyard and got

the stick. He wedged it into a space between two stones in the wall. The stick jutted out about four feet above the ground. The children took turns trying to hit the stick with a rock.

"Well done!" Richard cheered when John hit the stick three times in a row.

Anne and Henry managed to hit the stick once each. Richard and Ben missed every time.

"How'd you learn to throw like that?" Richard asked John.

"My brother, Francis, and I practice all the time in the back pasture," John said.

"Your father owns land?" Henry asked.

John nodded. "We have a farm."

"What are you doing in London?" Anne asked. "Where's your father?"

"He has business in Westminster," John answered. He didn't want to say anything about being lost in the city, so he added, "I'm meeting him later."

"Do you want to see a baby goat?"

Richard asked. "It was born last week."

John followed Anne and the boys down an alley. Just past another church, Henry pointed to a wood fence.

"In there," he said.

One by one, they squeezed past a broken board and entered a small muddy yard. A tan and white kid was tied to the fence. Richard and Henry began to pet it.

"Do you have goats on your farm?" Richard asked John.

John nodded. "My sister has one."

A man with white hair looked into the yard. He waved his arm.

"Get off with you all!" he yelled. "I don't want ruffians harming my goat."

"We're just petting it," Richard said.

"Get out, or I'll have the constable here for you!" The man picked up a broom and began shaking it at them.

"Let's go!" Anne said.

Giggling nervously, they pushed through the break in the fence and dashed up the street. Although no one was chasing them, they ran until they were breathless.

"Let's go to the market at Cheapside," Henry said.

A few minutes later they were ambling among the stalls of an open-air market. It seemed every food John could name was on sale—vegetables, fruit, meat, bread, honey, cheese. His stomach had never felt so empty.

"Hey, look!" Ben pointed to a baker balancing a tray of loaves. "Come on!"

With Ben in the lead, they gathered around the baker's stall as he transferred the loaves to a basket. The smell of the bread made John's mouth water.

"Thieves! Little thieves! Get the constable! They're stealing my bread!"

John's four companions darted off in four different directions. Someone grabbed him by the tunic. It was the baker, who continued to yell, "Constable!"

A crowd gathered near the baker's stall.

John heard a gruff voice. "I'm the constable here. Let me pass. Step back and let me through."

A man holding a constable's staff pushed his way through the crowd. "What's going on?" he asked the baker.

"This rascal and his gang came around again, stealing my goods," the baker said. "They stole from me last week too."

The constable scowled at John. "Did you pinch something from this baker?"

"No, I didn't," John answered.

"They all work together," the baker said. "Four or five of them come around, making noise and pushing, and the next thing you know, a loaf is missing."

"Were you with that bunch?" the constable asked John.

"Yes, but—"

"That's all I need to know," the constable said. He grabbed John with both hands. "It's off to the parish lockup with you. And then to the whipping post!"

# CHAPTER 6

"Please listen to me!" John begged. "I didn't know—"

"Silence!" the constable said. "Or you'll get yourself into a worse kettle of fish."

The crowd made way for the constable as he pulled John through the market. When they passed the last stall, a tall figure dressed from head to foot in black stepped in front of the constable.

"Signor Dandolo!" John cried.

Signor Dandolo inclined his head in

greeting and turned to the constable.

"Honored Constable," he said. "I am Signor Leonardo Dandolo, a Venetian merchant who has spent much time in your great country and is acquainted with your customs. I see that you have taken this boy into custody. With all the respect due to you, I must protest. This boy is neither ruffian nor vagrant and does not deserve harsh treatment."

The constable eyed Signor Dandolo's elegant hat and tunic. "You mean you know this miserable little scamp?"

"That is exactly my meaning. I met him and his esteemed father and brother today in the port."

"Well, I just met a baker," the constable said, "who swears his goods were pinched and this rogue was with the gang. Where is this esteemed father anyway?"

"He's doing business in Westminster," John answered. "I'm going to meet him later," he added.

"Since I am sure there has been some misunderstanding," Signor Dandolo responded, "please let me make amends to the baker and clear the boy's name."

The constable shrugged. "It's your coppers, so I suppose you can spend 'em as you please and save me some bother."

Signor Dandolo led the way back to the baker and paid for the missing loaf. Then the Venetian bought John two rolls.

"Thank you, Signor Dandolo," John said. "You saved me from the whipping post."

Signor Dandolo bowed. "I am grateful fortune brought us together again at the right moment. I regret only that I must hurry off. I am late for an appointment."

Signor Dandolo bowed again. "You must be careful in London. It is a city of wonders and opportunities. But there are many dangers as well."

John watched the tall figure merge into the traffic of the London street, the white plume of his hat bobbing gracefully.

His face is the only truly friendly one I've seen since morning, John thought. I wish he didn't have to hurry away.

Not knowing where to go or what else to do, John began to follow Signor Dandolo. While he walked, he ate the rolls. After ten or fifteen minutes, the neighborhood began to look familiar to him. Signor Dandolo was heading toward the Thames. In the distance, John saw the arches of London Bridge. The streets became even more crowded. John had to push and swerve around other people in order to move forward.

John lost sight of the Venetian near the bridge. He peered up and down the street and scanned the crowd climbing the stairs to the bridge. He saw no plumed black hat. But as he turned away, he caught sight of someone else on the stairs. Wavy black hair . . . a purple scar on the cheek.

John gasped. "Jennings!" He clenched

his fists. "Jennings, you swindler!"

Without thinking, John started after Jennings. He pushed his way up the stairs. Stumbling over feet, jabbing people by mistake, John got onto London Bridge. Lined with shops and houses, it spanned the Thames like a long crowded street.

Jennings was moving quickly. He slipped out of view several times, but John always found him again, rushing straight across the bridge. By the time Jennings reached the far side, John had managed to narrow the gap between them. Yet he was also careful to stay back a safe distance. Jennings descended from the bridge and immediately turned right.

"Excuse me, sir," John asked a workman on the stairs. "What's over there?" He pointed upriver—the direction in which Jennings was headed.

"The Southwark brick kilns," the man answered.

John continued to trail the swindler.

Jennings turned down a narrow lane and then ran down a deserted street along the water. From time to time, he paused in a doorway or peered around a corner.

"That lowlife! I know what he's doing!" John muttered. "He's stalking someone!"

Jennings stopped again. As he bent forward to look around a corner, he pulled something out of his tunic. John breathed in sharply when he saw what it was—a short stout stick with a metal head.

Jennings disappeared around the corner. An instant later, John heard his footsteps. He was running fast.

John dashed around the corner. In the deep shadows a dozen yards ahead, he saw two figures—Jennings and his victim. Jennings raised the stick and lunged at the other person.

"Signor Dandolo!" John screamed. "Watch out!"

# CHAPTER 7

Jennings swung the stick. The blow fell on Signor Dandolo's shoulder. He fell to his knees. Jennings bent over him and began to rip open his money bag. Signor Dandolo struggled. Jennings raised his stick high for a blow to the head.

John grabbed a broken brick from the ground. He aimed and hurled it as hard as he could. The brick hit Jennings in the knee. He staggered and toppled over.

"Signor Dandolo, get up! Fast!" John

yelled as he ran to the Venetian and helped him to his feet. Once he was standing, Signor Dandolo seemed to be all right. He and John hurried to the corner and then up the lane.

"Constable! Constable!" Signor Dandolo shouted.

John put two fingers in his mouth and whistled. A constable appeared at the end of the street. A second one joined him. Signor Dandolo and John led the officers to Jennings, who was still struggling to get up.

The constables seized Jennings and tied his hands behind his back.

"Well, well, just look who we've got here," one of them said. "If it isn't Nicholas Jennings himself, one of the worst thieves in all of London!"

"You scoundrel!" the other constable said. "We've been hunting you for months. You won't slip the law again. This time, you're caught for good!"

The constables thanked Signor Dandolo and John for catching the thief. Then they dragged him away.

Signor Dandolo and John walked side by side to a nearby square. At the public well, they rinsed their hands and faces and took long drinks of water. Signor Dandolo brushed off his velvet hat and tunic.

"So, *mio amico*," he said, "we meet again. We can never know what future the stars hold for us. It seems that you and I have been destined to share this day."

John looked at the Venetian's kind face and nodded.

Signor Dandolo reached inside the deep folds of his tunic and pulled out something. He held it in his closed hand and then opened his fingers.

John looked down and saw a round brass object with a glass top. Under the glass was a star decoration and an arrow. It wavered for a second and then was still.

"What is it?" John asked.

"This is a compass," Signor Dandolo said. "The arrow always points north. It was a gift from a Turkish sailor. I saved his life in Marseilles." He held the compass out to John. "Now I give it to you as a gift of thanks for the same reason—for saving my life. With this compass, you will never be lost."

John hesitated, then took the compass.

"Unfortunately," Signor Dandolo went on, "I must still attend to business. Much of the glass trade from Venice depends on what I do this evening."

"I wish you didn't have to go," John said. "Will I ever see you again?"

"Ah, who can say?" Signor Dandolo responded. "But if not, remember that you will be in my thoughts always."

Sweeping his plumed hat off his head, the Venetian bowed. *"Addio, amico mio."*

"Farewell," John said.

He leaned against the well. He pressed the compass in his hand. It felt smooth and cool. It seemed to say, Have no fear. When you are ready, I will help you find your way to new worlds.

John heard a distant sound. Drums, he thought.

"Can you tell me what those drums are?" he asked a woman who was filling a bucket at the well.

"It's the goings-on at Bankside," she answered. "That's just to the west of here."

"To the west," John murmured. "Maybe I can use the compass to find my way there."

He held out the compass. The arrow swung to the north. John faced west and began walking. As he moved along, he noticed that more and more people were going in the same direction. The drumming grew louder. The crowd became a procession.

It's as if we're all marching somewhere together, John thought. But where?

# CHAPTER 8

The rhythm of the drums gradually changed into music. Two instruments —a lute and a recorder—carried the merry tune. As the song became louder and more distinct, the crowd slowed down and then halted in front of a building.

It was three stories tall, oval in shape, with a sloping thatched roof. A banner flew over the roof, and another hung over the central doorway. Both banners carried the image of a single red blossom.

"It must be the Rose Theater that Father told us about," John exclaimed.

A man standing next to him laughed. "Well, there's a lad who's lucky enough to know where he's at. Bravo, my boy!"

Acrobats and jugglers were performing in front of the theater.

"Come one, come all to the finest entertainment in London town!" a crier shouted. "See children lost to a father and love found. Learn of shipwrecks and executions. Come one, come all to our *Comedy of Errors*!"

Along with hundreds of others, John moved toward the main door. As he neared the ticket sellers, he heard a familiar voice yelling, "John! John Smith of Lincolnshire!"

"Father!" John shouted. "Francis!"

A moment later, he was in his father's arms and hugging his brother.

"We searched for you all day!" his father scolded. "How could you let yourself get left behind? We've been worried sick." Mr. Smith sighed deeply. "But you're safe! I hoped you would remember I'd told you about the Rose Theater."

John couldn't speak. With one arm around Francis's waist, he pressed his head against his father's shoulder. He grinned at Francis. "Hey, I missed you, Sir Slugabed."

"How wonderful to be reunited!" their father said. "Shall we celebrate by seeing Mr. Shakespeare's play?"

John and Francis agreed. As they entered the theater, John slipped one of his hands into his father's. In the other hand, John clasped Signor Dandolo's compass and remembered the words, "You will be in my thoughts always."

❧

Pocahontas clasped the compass in her hand. The late afternoon sunlight still flickered on the water. She raised her eyes to where the clear blue of the sky met the deeper blue of the sea. Somewhere far beyond that horizon was London. And somewhere in London was John Smith.

"It's getting late," Thomas said. "I'd better get back to the fort."

Nakoma laughed. "How will you find it? You might get lost in the woods."

Thomas sighed. "That's no joke."

"I'm just teasing. We'll show you the way back. Right, Pocahontas?"

"To the fort?" Pocahontas murmured. "No, I'd like to stay here by myself for a while. But thank you for telling us the story, Thomas."

Nakoma and Thomas entered the woods. Pocahontas listened to their voices die away. The wind picked up. The ripples on the water became longer and deeper. They rolled toward her, one after the other. They rolled like the rhythmic beat of a drum, or like the voice of a friend saying, You will be in my thoughts always . . . always.